Believer

Book 1 of The Yuletide Tales

By Joseph M. Bubenik
Illustrated by Jeremy D. Plemon

Thank You

Author Thanks

I would like to thank Ben Wade, Brian Kennedy, Jake Feld, Travis Wagner, Joe Plemon, Spencer Bubenik, Bill Bubenik, Ben Bubenik, and my parents for reading early portions of this book and making me feel like it was worth continuing with.

A big thanks goes out to Jeremy Plemon for taking on this immense project and creating some really fun illustrations.

I'd like to especially thank L.B. Graham for taking the time to help me edit this story. He read the book at least twice, giving me detailed notes each time, which I found to be very helpful in creating a better book.

Finally, I'd like to thank my wife Ali. She put up with me spending lots of my free time with this story rather than her. She encouraged me and speaks well of me and my writing to others which makes me feel like I can succeed in this.

Illustrator Thanks

I would like to thank my wife Erin and my parents for their constant support. You guys rule.

Contents

The Waning Days of November

"Francis!" called a deep voice that was nearly lost among the sea of mutterings and murmurs coming from the other shoppers. Francis had once again gotten lost at the mall. It seemed like every holithey season the orphanage dragged him and the other boys to the mall, and every time some toy display distracted him. He would look up and the chaperones would be gone, replaced by a wall of strange adults. This year was no different.

He began to walk in the direction he thought the voice had come from, getting jostled from all sides. The voice grew louder as he neared the big department store, Gimbels. He passed mannequins wearing red sweaters and perfumed ladies using makeup pencils to therken eyebrows on prospective clients. He was nearing the huge Christmas tree in the center of the store, shimmering with tiny twinkling lights.

Oddly, the voice seemed to be coming from the tree itself. Why would anyone be in the tree? The mall security guard had chastised Francis for the very same thing last year. Maybe it was okay this year? Francis circled the tree trying to see someone within the bedecked limbs but failed to see anyone anywhere within.

"Hello?" Francis called out to the voice. The voice once again spoke his name. It was coming from the tree most definitely. Francis squinted his eyes, searching every opening. A little up to the left – was that ornament glowing slightly?

As Francis' focus locked onto the glowing red ball thengling from a branch of the fir tree, his eyes flew open wide. There on the ornament was Santa's face staring back at him. Stranger still, the face began to speak, a deep resonant voice filling Francis' head. "Francis, you must come to the North Pole. Tothey. Christmas is in thenger of being ended forever."

"Santa?" Francis asked the ornament in confusion.

"Yes, my boy. I need you to find the storage room and go out the door to the loading dock."

"Santa Claus?"

"Francis, I realize this may be a surprise for you, especially seeing that you stopped believing in me last year, but there is no time to thewdle! You yourself are in grave thenger. It has taken me a long time to locate you, and I believe Rauhen has

9

learned of your whereabouts as well. His agents have entered the mall that you are giving your patronage. They are searching for you. You must find the loading dock quickly. My man Crosby is there, waiting for you."

"Why didn't you bring me any – "

"Hush! There is no time. I feel his agents. Run!"

Francis turned to see two large men enter Gimbel's, hunched over, their gait somewhat reminiscent of gorillas. They were wearing parkas with the hoods pulled up, scarves covering their faces. Amber eyes scanned through the crowd. They were wearing white fur gloves. No, not gloves. Their hands were covered in white fur, their fingers tipped with jagged black claws.

Their eyes locked on him.

Deafening bellows filled the air, more animal than human, quickly followed by the shrieks of the other customers. The men began an ape-like charge towards Francis, pushing people roughly out of their way and tossing others high in the air as they plowed forward.

"Run!" Santa shouted and Francis did.

Francis ran, knocking over his fair share of people in his own haste to get away. As he ran, he scanned the back wall of the store and saw a door marked "Employees Only." He bolted towards it. He threw open the door and slipped in, slamming the door behind him and locking it.

"Hey! You can't be in here," a heavy set man declared as he grabbed Francis roughly by the arm. His next sentence trailed off when the door splintered under the pressure of a massive white-furred fist. The second crash made the man loosen his hold on Francis, who promptly left the man behind as he sprinted towards the exit.

Standing in the cold night air was a short, stout man, wearing clothes of therk green fur. He had a large hammer strapped to his back and a jagged scar crossing his right eye. The eye beneath the scar was gone, replaced with red glass, similar to the red ornament in which Francis had seen Santa. Behind him was the biggest reindeer Francis had ever seen, eight feet tall at the shoulders, muscles clearly visible beneath the skin. An intricately decorated leather saddle was fastened to the beast's back. When they saw him, the reindeer kneeled down and the short man quickly climbed up onto his back.

"Up, lad! We no time for talk!" the man shouted. Francis sprinted towards them. The man grasped him under his armpit and yanked him up into the saddle behind himself. "Yah!" he shouted and the reindeer took off quickly, just as the two huge men exploded into the night air. They gave chase, but as the reindeer picked up speed they left the ground and climbed into the chill night sky.

The Blustering Winds
of The North

"Who were those men?" Francis shouted above the whooshing wind.

"'What were them 'things?' be a better question," the man who must have been Crosby shouted back. He had a peculiar way of speaking; it reminded Francis of what an old pirate might sound like. "They be snowmen. Abominable Snowmen. Nasty things, when they get ahold of ya. Took out me eye, one of them did. Fortunately he left me my mitts, one good eye, and ol' Ironhead here," he said as he patted the head of his hammer. "He won't be bothering no one else."

With that explanation, the man grew quiet, and they sat mutely as the wind whistled around them. Millions of questions raced through Francis' mind as he held onto the back of Crosby, but they passed too quickly for him to be able to voice any particular query. So, he watched the ground pass by them at a surprising speed. They were still climbing into the air when one question stuck out to Francis, and he blurted out, "Are you an elf?"

"Some call us that, others say we're northmen. Makes no matter to me. I know ya have odd notions of us down in the south, but we be just like your own men; maybe a bit shorter and we's want to wear beards on account of the cold."

"Do you make toys?"

"Aye, some of us do, but not me. Santa's got other uses for me. There's a war going on, has been for years. Many of us have had to take up our tools to protect the workshop rather than build toys in it."

Francis considered what he had heard. Then he asked the question that had be niggling at his mind for some time, just finally making itself clear: "Why did Santa say he's been searching for me for a long time?"

"He been searching for someone for a long time. Not so sure you's the boy he needs. Most of us don't think you is the one. But, if'n Santa says to fetch ya, I do what he says. If ya ain't the one, I'll take ya back, maybe knock ya on the head to help ya 'forget' 'bout all this. Word to the wise: when I take ya back, it'll go better for ya if ya don't tell no one about all this. They'll just think yer crazy, anyway."

Francis was mulling over what the ramifications would be if he was indeed the one Santa was looking for, when he heard a faint keening sound coming from behind them. He turned around and far off in the distance he noticed several glowing specks that seemed to be growing larger at a swift rate. As they grew nearer, their glow took on a misty purple appearance. "What are those?" Francis asked Crosby, pointing behind them.

Crosby turned and his face drained of color. He slapped the reins down hard and gave a shout. The reindeer seemed to double his efforts. And yet the glowing things still seemed to be gaining on them, whining and wailing all the way.

"What's wrong?" Francis shouted through the wind.

"Humbugs!" Crosby shouted back.

Talking was difficult through the wind, and Crosby seemed preoccupied with what he was doing so Francis turned to get a better look at these 'Humbugs' as they approached. Their wails were decidedly eerie. As they neared, their forms became clearer. Twisted human shapes, whose midsections trailed off to mist rather than legs. Their arms were reaching out for Francis. Their mouths were closed, but they still whined and wailed in a most disturbing fashion. They seemed... discontented. That was the best way Francis could think to describe it. He also decided he wished to avoid any type of social interaction with them.

"What are we going to do; they're gaining on us!" Francis shouted.

"Don't ya think I know that?!" Crosby retorted. "I'm taking us to that grove of fir trees up there. It's one of the safe havens Santa and Present made. Humbugs can't go in the circle of trees, powerful magic protects these sanctuaries."

Up ahead, Francis saw a stand of Christmas trees, covered in candles and red and gold ornaments. He looked behind them and saw that the Humbugs appeared to be closer to them than they were to the grove. With nothing to do but hold on, Francis became decidedly nervous.

The first Humbug soon came close enough to reach out for Francis. Francis swung a fist at the ghoul, but his arm passed right through as if nothing were there.

Francis felt colder than he ever had before while he touched the thing, cold and resentful. Oddly, the Humbug let out a shriek and backed away when Francis swung through it.

They were almost to the stand of trees when another Humbug came up and touched the reindeer's hind leg. There was a hideous rending sound and the mount and its riders began falling towards the ground. Francis saw that they were going to land within the circle of trees. Sure enough, the Humbugs pulled away, their piteous whining noises going with them.

Francis turned to look at the ground in just enough time to see the snow come up to greet them.

3 The Landing & the Watchers

Francis' consciousness slowly crept back into wakefulness. His head hurt. The sky was still therk, but circling the grove of Christmas trees some twenty feet up were those purple glowing things. Francis jerked back as he noticed them, but then remembered that they could not enter the stand of trees. He watched them as they hung motionlessly in the air, their eyes fixed on him.

After Francis decided that they truly were not going to come in, he pulled himself out of the snowdrift he had landed in. He gingerly took a few tentative steps, checking for broken bones.

Assuring himself that he was in one piece, Francis walked over to where Crosby was just sitting up, rubbing his neck and grumbling about wishing he could wring the neck of "one of them poisonous purple wind bags."

"What exactly is a 'Humbug'?!" Francis inquired, none too composed, pointing up at the hovering ring of ominous watchers.

Crosby eyed him for a long moment before speaking: "Help me with Blitzen." He rose sluggishly and tottered over to where the reindeer lay, whimpering to itself. The reindeer seemed to be in one piece, but where the ghoul had touched him was an unsettling purple haze. Crosby gingerly moved the leg around as Blitzen whined. "Nothing's broken, but I be guessing the muscles around here be all twisted and torn."

"Well I'm glad his leg's not broken," Francis said, irritated at being ignored, "but what is a Humbug? Are there other things I need to look out for? Coal monsters? Deranged polar bears? Heat Miser?!"

Crosby glared at him. "For one who's probably not even supposed to be up here, I've told ya plenty. But if ya must know, Humbugs are born whenever one of you southron folks gives up on love and joy at Christmas. When you stop keeping Christmas in yer heart, yer heart dies a bit and that death slowly manifests into one of them," Crosby said pointing at the Humbugs. "They don't talk, they don't feel, they just hate."

Francis stewed in frustration. How was he supposed to act? He had just been minding his own business when he started hearing voices, huge goons had tried to kill him, and he had been pulled onto a flying reindeer by a rude, short man. Exasperated, Francis grabbed a branch from the ground and hurled it at one of the Humbugs. It passed harmlessly through, and the glowing purple presence did not seem to register the affront. It just kept staring at Francis.

"How do we get out of here?" Francis asked. He had been angry at his situation, not knowing why Santa wanted him and being oddly offended at the notion that Crosby didn't think he was worthy. But now, staring at the ghostly sentinels all around him, he was feeling ashamed that people he knew could have been responsible for these monsters. Maybe even him.

Crosby noticed the change in Francis' demeanor and offered, "Nothing to worry about. They'll go when the sun rises. They can't seem to stand it, too joyous maybe. Until then, we can sleep some and then busy ourselves with getting Blitzen up and ready to walk. With his hind leg hurt like that, I can't imagine he'll be up to flying, let alone carrying us. I think we're a couple safe havens away from the North Pole. We'll have to travel fast to reach the next one by nightfall."

They did their best to make Blitzen comfortable, then laid down next to him. He was a large animal, so there was plenty of room for both them to lean against him, each sharing their warmth with the others. Francis was exhausted and soon drifted off into sleep, the purple sentinels nearly forgotten.

The Snow That Lasts Forever

It had been a difficult day of hiking through the northern wilderness. Francis wasn't used to long treks through snow like Crosby was. On top of that, Blitzen needed continual encouragement to keep going. He had a horrible limp and was mewling constantly from pain. Francis and Crosby took turns tugging on his reigns.

They had stopped only once for a short rest. Fortunately, Crosby had some gingerbread cookies in his coat pocket that they ate sparingly.

Francis had learned long ago at the orphanage that complaining got you nothing, except maybe a shove. He kept his hunger and discomfort to himself, especially seeing how determined Crosby was to make it to the next sanctuary by dusk. Francis' memories of the Humbugs helped keep him moving as well

It was late afternoon when the grove of trees came into sight. The sun was still mostly above the horizon. The promise of safety gave Francis a newfound energy, and as Crosby was leading Blitzen, he took off towards the decorated trees. He had not made it ten paces when he stumbled over something underneath the snow. As he had been running so fast, he landed face first in the snow. He heard Crosby laughing as he got up and brushed the snow from his face and clothes.

In his embarrassment, he went to pick up the object that had tripped him so he could toss it at Crosby. As he cleared the snow away, his anger melted into curiosity; a handsomely carved wooden box, stained a deep red with forest green accents lay beneath a blanket of snow. He looked up to see Crosby standing still with his mouth agape. "What?" Francis asked the incredulous looking elf.

"That what ya tripped over?" he hesitantly asked.

"Yeah, you saw me. I was running and then I tripped over this dumb box because someone left it under the snow." Francis sounded more upset than he truly was. He was very interested in this box, especially seeing how Crosby was reacting to it. The elf was just standing there, staring at the box. He barely even blinked. Hadn't he seen a wooden box before?

Francis' interest in the box overcame his intrigue at Crosby's dumbfounded response. He opened the box to find that it was lined with satin. Nestled in the fabric was a single Christmas light bulb. A tad more than an inch long, it was green in color. "Weird," Francis remarked aloud. "Why would anyone keep one light bulb in such a nice box?"

Francis picked up the bulb and dropped it in surprise: as soon as he touched the bulb, it had begun to glow. He looked up at Crosby, whose eyes now seemed to be bulging out in surprise. Somewhat hesitantly, Francis reached down again and picked the bulb up. It did glow. Francis held the bulb up high. It shown brightly against the therkening sky.

Francis' enjoyment of the moment was shattered by far off whining that carried over the wind. Francis and Crosby, shaken from their amazed stupor, looked behind them to see a purple glow coming upon them. Francis dropped the bulb and it shattered on a patch of ice. In his haste to make it to safety, he dropped the box and began to run.

"No, ya fool!" Crosby shouted. "Take the box; it be yer future!"

Francis stopped and looked at Crosby. His desire for safety warred with his intrigue over the box. Finally, he returned for the box. Crosby and Blitzen had caught up to him by now. They all three raced for the safety of the trees.

They were almost to the grove when Crosby shouted for Francis to go ahead into the grove. Blitzen was dragging now, even attempting to lie down. Five feet from the safety of the trees, Blitzen collapsed.

Crosby closed his eyes and took a deep breath. He stood, and in a deep, gruff baritone began to sing some old carol that Francis had never heard. It was simple and sad sounding, requesting a savior to come. As he continued to sing, he turned and pulled his hammer from over his shoulder. Curiously, Crosby began to take on a golden shimmer. He finished the verse just before the Humbugs were upon him. He let out a fierce bellow and swung his great hammer at the lead Humbug and there was a blinding flash of light. Francis shielded his eyes.

When his vision returned, the Humbugs were gone. Crosby was breathing heavily, furiously trying to push Blitzen. He seemed drained. Francis ran out to them and together they got the mighty reindeer within the circle of trees.

Once in, Crosby collapsed next to Blitzen, snoring loudly.

5 Christmas Eve The Year Before

"Santa's not real, you freak!" Francis' bunk mate at the orphanage shouted down from his top bunk.

"But what proof do you have, BZ?" Francis asked.

"Proof?! Oh man, you're hopeless. Leave me alone. The other guys are starting to give me a hard time just for talking to you." BZ told Francis.

Every year Francis had this argument with the other boys at the orphanage. Only BZ was even remotely cordial to Francis, and that was because they shared a bunk bed. It was becoming more and more difficult to keep his faith in Santa, and the Christmas spirit in general, when his peers disparaged him so mercilessly. "What about all the presents we get on Christmas?" Francis asked BZ.

"All the presents? Come on, Francis, those are donations from the thrift store down the street. They're never even wrapped. They're dirty and broken – leftovers and after thoughts. You think Santa is bringing us this junk? Man, you really are delusional. I'd be more inclined to believe in Santa if we got coal."

Francis decided to let the matter rest. The other boys would see. Santa never truly let them down. Tomorrow morning there would be loads of presents for each of them. There had to be. And BZ would stand with Francis against the other boys. He would finally have a real friend. After all these years of never knowing his parents and never feeling like he belonged, it was only a few short hours of sleep until his life of one would expand drastically to two.

Francis did his best to fall asleep quickly, but the excitement of the special they kept him awake. Finally, unsure if he had ever even fallen asleep, Francis saw the glimmer of the rising sun peaking through the blinds of the nearest window.

Francis bolted upright. He jumped out of bed and began shaking the other boys in his room: "Wake up! It's Christmas!" The other boys sat up slowly, clearly lacking the vigor he had for this morning. Some even grumbled about being woken up so early. Grumbled!

Francis ran out of the room and down the hall. He took the steps two at a time; he beat everyone else down to the tiny, shabby tree the orphanage kept for the boys. Sure enough, there were all kinds of things surrounding the tree.

But wait... none of the items were wrapped. Well, no matter. Gifts were gifts, wrapping or not.

They did indeed look dirty and worn, just as BZ had said... Well, toys were still toys, even if another kid had played with them first.

By now, the other boys had trickled down into the main room. Presents were being divvied up. It was starting to look like each boy had one gift with his name on it. The pile was getting more and more sparse as Francis looked for his gift. Harold had gotten a baseball glove. Walter, a set of miniature race cars.

Fewer and fewer gifts remained.

Pete got a furry hat. Roger got a pogo stick. BZ got a carved statue of an alligator.

They all received something, even though most of the boys were not interested in what they got. They all did, except Francis. Santa must've forgotten him...

All of the boys quietly looked at Francis. A few had smug grins on their faces. Francis looked at BZ, hoping that they would still be friends. His bunk-mate stared at him for a moment, then walked towards him. He looked Francis in the eye.

"I told you he doesn't exist."

The Glowing Bulb

The night passed easier than the previous one. Francis trusted the safety of the trees and was able to sleep soundly the entire night, even with the Humbugs hovering around the perimeter. Francis awoke refreshed to the smell of cooking meat and smoke. Crosby had managed to catch a wild hare in the pre-dawn gloom and was roasting it over a cook fire.

As they were eating, Francis picked up the box that Crosby was so adamant he keep. It was sturdily built; it showed no signs of weakening, even after he had dropped it in his haste to make it to the trees. The corners did not look chipped, nor were the edges worn. A fine box, Francis decided. Too bad that bulb had broken when he dropped it. It was a neat trick, the bulb glowing in his hand like that. The boys at the home would have definitely been impressed if he could have shown them that trick. He might have even made a friend with that trick. A real…

Francis had opened the box as he was thinking about the boys at the orphanage. Resting upon the satin cloth was a light bulb, just like the other one, but this one was blue. But there had only been a single bulb in the box before, and it had been green. Francis looked up at Crosby quizzically. The elf just gave him a knowing smile and continued eating his haunch of rabbit leg. Crosby's shock over the box must have receded. He was not even surprised that a new bulb had shown up.

Francis picked up the bulb, and it too began to glow. He closed the box and opened it again.

Empty.

He set the box down and stood up. He took a step and slid across the ground as if on ice skates. He wobbled as he regained his balance. He held the bulb up. It still glowed. "What is going on?" Francis wondered aloud. He took another step, and more gracefully this time, slid across the ground.

When he came to stop, he set the bulb down on the ground. Cautiously he took another step. The ground was no longer slick as ice. Francis stared at the dark bulb he had left on the ground a step away. A smile spread across his face as a thought occurred to him. He snatched the bulb up and took two quick steps, hoping that he would glide across the ground.

It worked! He began pumping his legs faster and faster, laughing as he got the hang of it. He zoomed around the grove, finally coming to a stop in front of Crosby. "This is so cool! Do you know what this box is?"

"Aye," Crosby acknowledged through his beard.

"Well...?" Francis asked the elf.

"Not me place to tell ya the secrets of the Gift."

"You're just a spoiled sport because I found this awesome box and you didn't," Francis informed Crosby. Francis circled around Crosby, sticking his tongue out and making taunting sounds until he hit an odd bump on the ground. He windmilled his arms in the air, trying to regain his balance. Snowballs flew from his right hand, which was not holding the light bulb. Crosby roared with laughter as Francis fell to the ground. Without even thinking about what he was doing, Francis flung his hand at Crosby and from nowhere, a snowball pelted Crosby in the face.

Crosby's laughter ceased as Francis as guffawed.

Crosby brushed his face and beard off and lunged for Francis, who was too quick for him. Francis was laughing hysterically as he skated away from Crosby, pelting him with endless snowballs. Once, when Crosby was close, Francis tried to fling a snowball from his left hand, accidentally throwing the light bulb, which broke on Crosby's chest. Francis began to stumble as he no longer slid on the ground.

Crosby tackled the boy to the ground. As they landed, both boy and elf burst into laughter, which woke the reindeer. Blitzen snorted angrily at being woken and shifted himself to face the opposite direction as the new friends' merriment continued.

The Puzzle of the Empty Box

After they finished their meal and got Blitzen up and ready to move, Francis checked inside his wooden box again. Sure enough, a new bulb was nestled within: a red one. He took it out and closed the box. Then he opened the box as quickly as he could to see if there was some sort of mechanism he was not noticing.

"It be magic, boy," Crosby called to Francis from the far side of the hobbling reindeer.

"So now you want to tell me about my box, is that it?" Francis replied.

"No, that's Santa's job. Just didn't want ya wasting yer time trying to figure out how the Gift works."

Francis tucked the box beneath one arm and examined the glowing red bulb with the other as they hiked. It wasn't particularly blindingly bright, but it was definitely noticeably shining. When he held the blue bulb, he had noticed its power as soon as he took his first step. This red bulb was not so easily figured out. He had tried taking a sliding step, but that only caused him to stumble. He flung his arm as if he were throwing a snowball, yet nothing happened. He eyed Crosby, who always seemed to have a knowing smile on his face. Francis turned away from the elf and kept walking.

An hour or so later, Francis made a discovery: he wasn't cold. Normally by this time of their theily treks, his feet would be freezing and he would have to keep his gloveless hands in his pockets. One hand was holding the bulb and the other was wrapped around the Gift. They felt positively toasty. His feet might even be sweating, though he didn't deem it necessary to take his shoes off to see.

To test his discovery, Francis placed the bulb back into the empty box. As soon as he closed the lid, he was bitterly cold. He hurriedly grabbed the bulb out of the box and immediately felt comfortably warm again.

That afternoon when they reached the grove, Francis made a decision: he would see how many bulbs this box would give him and what they did. It seemed like the box only provided a new bulb when the previous one had been broken. He had tried to hide one to see if the box would give him a second, but the box seemed to know. He would have to break this bulb... but not until the fire was good and warm.

After dinner, Francis pondered breaking the bulb. It seemed a waste to merely just smash it. He thought about it for a time until he had a great idea.

Francis quietly scooped up a handful of snow. He fashioned it into a snowball around the red bulb and hurled it at Crosby's face. In a flash, Crosby had his hammer out and swatted the snowball away.

"So that be how it is, eh?" Crosby muttered to himself.

He calmly walked over to Francis who was a little disconcerted by Crosby's serious manner. Before Francis could react, Crosby picked him up and stuffed him head first into a tall drift of snow. "Bet ya wish ya had that red bulb now, don't ya?" Crosby called to Francis as he strolled back to his seat laughing. "You may indeed be the one Santa be looking for, but there's no need for me to treat ya like royalty."

The Growing Things

Francis spent the rest of the night trying to warm himself by the fire. He did indeed wish he hadn't broken the red bulb so hastily. Any time he looked at Crosby, the gruff elf's face broke into a broad smile. "It's good to mind yer betters," Crosby jovially informed Francis.

"I thought you looked a little warm, that's why I threw the snowball," Francis said with a grin.

"Were that the reason, now?" Crosby had a good laugh and got up. He walked over to the wounded reindeer, laid down, and soon was snoring soundly. After enjoying the warmth of the fire for a while longer, Francis walked over to Crosby and nudged him with his foot.

"What did you mean when you said I was the one Santa was looking for?"

"Couldn't of asked me that before I went to sleep?" Crosby gruffly complained. "Ya got the Gift now, boy. Not everyone finds a magic box like thet. Or are ya so used to magic boxes that it didn't seem like a big deal?" Crosby gave him a smile, then turned back to sleep. Still somewhat confused, Francis lay down and soon joined them, finding the reindeer's side to be quite comfortable…

Francis once again woke up to the smell of cooking meat. He sat up and looked at the sleeping Blitzen. "Ol' Blitzen ain't doin' s'good," Crosby solemnly informed Francis. "We may needs stay here tothey so that he can rest." Francis looked at Blitzen's wounded leg. Although not immediately apparent under the fur, Blitzen's leg was indeed red and swollen.

"Poor guy," Francis quietly said to Blitzen as he patted his neck. "I hope some rest is just what you need." With that, Francis got up and went to have breakfast. The meal was good as Crosby seemed to have some understanding of the local plants and how they could be used to season wild game. They did not talk much, worry over Blitzen filling their minds.

By late morning, Francis was really ready to open his box, hoping to find a new bulb: it was a green one once again. Although he had the green bulb first, he had not had an opportunity to find out what power this one might bestow.

He picked up the bulb and it began to glow familiarly. He tried taking a step, trying to see if it would affect his walking; no change. He stood still to see if he felt any differently: he felt the same.

Francis began to ponder about the powers the bulbs had given him. The blue bulb had given him control over the winter elements, whereas the red bulb had given him some sort of connection to warmth. Holding the green bulb in his hand, Francis looked up and saw the green needles of the trees encircling them. Francis smiled to himself and walked over to the nearest tree and placed his hand on the trunk.

A rush of understanding filled Francis' head as he instantly knew the tree. He knew each fiber, each needle, each branch and knot. He knew what the tree had seen in its life. He knew where the tree could bend and where it would break. He could feel how this tree and presumably the others were imbued with magic to create a safe place from Rauhen and his minions. Francis not only knew this tree, he was this tree. He reached out through one of the tree's branches and picked up Crosby by his collar. The startled elf began shouting immediately, hurling insults at his unseen attacker.

Crosby calmed hastily at the sound of Francis' laughter. "Ye be getting yerself in all sorts of trouble with that box," he snarled. With a smooth twist of his shoulder, Crosby slipped out of his coat and dropped to his feet on the ground. Before Francis could respond, he was once again head first in a pile of snow.

9

The Raising of the Ring

Francis dug himself out of the snow drift and began following Crosby around their camp, looking for ways to help out. Crosby busied himself with checking his travel pack, sharpening his knife, and generally trying to fill up the day with labor.

Francis learned lots about the great northern wilderness from Crosby that day. He taught Francis which patches of snow were best to walk on, which berries could be eaten, and how to find the best wood for a fire, among other things.

Crosby told great stories about growing up in the North Pole. He talked about getting chased by a polar bear when he was only an elfling. He told a story of how he stowed away on Santa's sleigh his first year working at the workshop. He talked about how Rauhen had not existed when he was born over 300 years ago.

With all the work and stories, the day seemed to pass quickly. Crosby checked on Blitzen frequently, but he was unsure whether or not the reindeer was gaining any strength.

In the late afternoon it began to snow heavily. Francis used his green lightbulb to move the tree branches so that they formed a pine pavilion over them. It was pleasant to sit by the fire and look out at the falling snow. They went to bed early, as they planned on getting started on their trek as soon as the sun rose the next morning.

In the morning, Francis and Crosby woke and ate a breakfast of leftovers from the previous day. Blitzen was sluggish to rise, panting in a pained manner when he finally got to his feet. They gave the huge beast some water and some barley Crosby had in his pack. They began their trip shortly thereafter.

Traveling with the injured reindeer was even slower than before; they had to help him to his feet several times an hour. It was an exhausting day. By early afternoon, Francis was getting anxious about reaching the next sanctuary in time for nightfall. He mentioned his concern to Crosby, but the elf merely grunted and plodded on.

A few hours later, with the sun sinking behind the horizon, the ghostly moan began again behind them. The Humbugs were too far away to be seen, but they were coming. Crosby patted Blitzen on the shoulder. The reindeer took the cue and collapsed on the ground. Crosby dropped his pack and reached for his hammer.

Realization of what was happening dawned in Francis' mind. For a moment he panicked. He rushed to Crosby, grabbing the coat sleeve in a tight grip, but he was too scared to think of anything to say.

"Not a time for letting fear control ya, boy," Crosby muttered to Francis. "I need ya to think."

Francis let go of Crosby's sleeve and tried to think. The situation seemed hopeless, and Francis was soon grasping Crosby's sleeve once again. He began hyperventilating until Crosby slapped him soundly across the face, then grabbed his shirt collar, pulling Francis' face within inches of his own. "NOT a time for letting fear control ya," Crosby growled at Francis. "I told ya to think!"

Francis stared at the bearded elf, his mind blank. Crosby let Francis go, took a deep breath, and began to sing some ancient song and turned to face the now visible ghouls. He did not seem to glow as quickly as he had before. In fact, Crosby seemed almost pained as he sang, as if each word were an effort to pronounce.

Suddenly, a thought occurred to Francis: He ran to a nearby tree and pulled a branch off. He hurried back to Crosby and the reindeer and stuck the branch in the ground. Then, holding the bulb in one hand, he grasped the tiny branch and became one with it. He remembered how the other sanctuary trees were created.

Francis focused, believing that this branch was the same size and shape and made for the same purpose as the trees from the sanctuaries.

The tiny branch quivered in the ground, then shot into the air, growing in girth as it grew in height. Fresh green shoots shot out of the side of the trunk, growing bark and then sprouting needles. Red and gold sap began oozing from pores on the limbs, oozing until they formed perfectly round and shiny ornaments. Soft popping sounds announced the appearance of tiny lights blinking on among the needles.

"Hurry up, lad, one tree don't give us much protection."

Francis took the suggestion to heart and grabbed several more small branches. He began placing them in the ground in a rough circle around Crosby, Blitzen, and himself. After he placed each, he touched it and believed it was as the first.

After his first bundle had become full grown trees, he grabbed another bunch and began filling in among the others.

"I did it!" Francis shouted.

"Ya got to link them," Crosby shouted at the boy.

Confused, Francis reached out and grabbed a branch from the nearest tree. It was true. The trees were not linked like the ones at the other circles.

With the Humbugs bearing down on them, Francis grabbed a branch from the nearest tree in his other hand and linked them. He created the link between each tree until the circle was complete, with only seconds to spare. Humbugs slammed into the protective barrier, screeching in protest. Francis stumbled back in shock, knocking the elf over. "This be yer way of getting back at me for last night?"

"S-s-s-sorry," Francis said, trying to come up with a response. After a few moments, he let out a relieved sigh. Francis lay down on the ground as the Humbugs moaned above them.

178 Years Ago

Crosby had never enjoyed making toys, but it wasn't like there was much else to do at the workshop: There were plenty of elves on reindeer duty already. He felt even less inclined to work in the textile section of the shop, and though he was secretly interested in working in the bakery, he knew his skills were rudimentary at best. Working there, he would likely only make children detest Christmas cookies and candies.

"Hey, Croz," a shorter, rounder elf called, "You mind giving me a hand with this log?"

"Aye, Ives. Let me get this peg in place first."

Crosby hurriedly shoved a wooden peg into its hole, pinning a wheel to the side of a wagon, then walked over to Ives who was struggling to get a large section of tree into place. Crosby gently moved Ives aside and picked up the log by himself, placing it gingerly onto the waiting sawhorses. "Thanks, Croz, that would've taken me ages to get up there myself." Ives looked approvingly at the log, then changed topics: "What have you got planned for the evening?"

"Nothing fancy, maybe catch a glimpse of Merry before her Da makes her come in for the night," he told his friend.

"Ah, young love," Ives melodramatically whispered.

Crosby promptly punched him in the shoulder. Ives laughed and said, "It's no secret you want to marry her, Croz. I think you should just elf up and ask her."

Crosby stared at his friend and thought maybe he was right for a change. He gave Ives a smile and walked back to his own station. When the bells rang to signal the end of the shift, Crosby cleaned up his station and bid a good night to his friends. He grabbed his tools, thinking he might make something for Merry in his free time tonight and headed out into the cold night.

He took a path that brought him near the textile workshop, hoping to catch Merry on her way out. As luck would have it, she and a few of her friends were leaving the shop just as he was walking by. She caught sight of him and smiled, but looked away quickly. Crosby's face turned red and he smiled back, even though she was no longer looking at him. Crosby caught up and silently walked with them.

They had entered the main square of town when Merry noticed a purple glow slowly drifting towards them from the sky. She stopped and watched the glowing thing approach. The others stopped when she did and then noticed the thing as well. It was moaning piteously.

When it landed some thirty feet in front of them, Merry stepped towards it. Crosby reached to grab her arm, but she gave him a look with a hint of a smile in her eyes. "Be careful, lass," he told her. She began walking towards the thing and Crosby followed a few steps behind.

"Are you hurt?" Merry called to whatever it was floating in front of them. It continued to moan, but did reach out for her. "See, Crosby, the poor thing is hurt and needs help." She walked up to the thing and reached for its outstretched hand. The moment their fingers touched, a scream burst from her lips but was silenced as the other of the thing's hands touched her shoulder. She collapsed.

The girls burst into shrieks of terror as Crosby stood there momentarily stunned. The thing had lost contact with her when she fell, but it slowly floated to the ground and touched her cheek.

As one of the girls fainted, Crosby began running to Merry. He hurled his toolbox at the thing, but it just passed right through. Crosby was going to tackle the thing, but he stopped dead in his tracks when it looked away from Merry and right at him. It didn't seem to move fast, but Crosby didn't think it would be wise to touch it.

They stared at each other.

Then Crosby lunged for Merry. He grabbed one of her ankles and pulled her away from the thing. As he scooped her up off of the ground, he heard a loud commotion coming from behind him. As he turned and ran with Merry, he saw that many elves had come when they heard the screaming. Santa was stepping out of the main workshop when Crosby ran past it. Santa called to Crosby, but more screams were coming from behind him. Crosby just kept running.

- - - - - - - - - - - - - - - - - -

"Brought her back to her Da," Crosby finished.

"Was she okay?" Francis asked.

Crosby's eyes glistened as he ignored the question. A few silent moments passed, leading Francis to believe the conversation was over. Crosby rolled over in the dark, tugging his coat up to his chin. "I never had me a wife or elflings to focus on. Spent me life fighting the darkness, protecting Claus, protecting Christmas," Crosby whispered. "I'd do anything to keep Christmas as it is."

"Night, lad," Crosby said.

The sun rose the next morning, but Blitzen could not. His flesh was hot to the touch and he barely seemed lucid. Francis and Crosby sat in silence. "It be time, boy," Crosby quietly informed Francis. "Blitzen be in too much pain to go on."

"What are you saying?" Francis asked. "We can't just leave him here by himself."

"Not living, no."

"You're going to kill him?!" Francis exclaimed.

"It be a mercy for me friend. He can't make it to the stable, and I won't leave him to die slowly. He deserves better than that." Crosby began walking towards the reindeer, unslinging his hammer as he went.

Francis raced passed Crosby and threw himself on the wounded animal. Crosby and Blitzen had been the two constants in his life since this whirlwind of change had begun several theys before. He couldn't lose one of the only two friends he had in the entire world. He wrapped his arms around the beast's neck and his tears sunk into Blitzen's fur. "It's not fair!" Francis wailed, "It shouldn't be like this!"

"I know, lad. I know."

"It SHOULDN'T be like this." Francis stood up and shouted to the sky. He jumped up and down and kicked at a drift of snow. Finally, he stood still and hoped, prayed, wished... believed that it was different.

A bright flash of golden light startled Francis, and he fell on his behind. A deep resonant laugh filled the air. Francis looked behind him and was startled to see a giant man, most of ten feet tall, with fiery red hair and beard. He had a wreath of holly leaves on his head and a red fur coat that went all the way to the ground.

"You've done well, Francis," the big man exclaimed as he picked Francis up by one hand and placed him on his feet. He laughed loudly as he saw Francis' bewildered face. "Crosby, I see that you are well." As soon as he finished speaking, he was laughing again. It seemed that if he was not speaking, he was laughing.

"Aye, Present, I been worse, tis true," Crosby responded to the giant.

"The only one with problems seems to be poor Blitzen. Got a touch of the Humbugs, did he now?" More boisterous laughter.

"Crosby says he's not going to make it," Francis lamented to the joyful man.

"Oh, that would be true, that would be true..." a small chuckle, "except for you. I'm surprised you did not even need the aid of the focus to reach out to me."

"Reach out to you? Who are you? How did I reach out to you?"

The man laughed loudly at the stream of questions. "You did indeed call to me with your belief that things should be different. I am the Ghost of Christmas Present. I reside in the here and now, and my purpose is to make things more as they should be. When you know that things should be different, I feel that need."

"You're here to make things better? You mean you're going to make the Humbugs and snowmen and Rauhen disappear?" Francis asked.

For a moment, Present's face was sad. "Oh, if only my power was that great. I am bound by the here and now. Even if all the Humbugs and snowmen were here now, I doubt I would be able to stop them all. You see, my power is directed by the belief of a few special individuals. If you were able to face the vast hordes of Rauhen's legions and believe them to be no more, maybe... maybe. But that would take an enormous amount of belief."

"So you're saying you can't do anything?" Francis looked down at the ground and began to cry. He was shaken from his tears by still more laughter. He looked up to see the big man walking over to the dying reindeer.

"Fortunately your belief that this beast should live is stronger than your faith in me!" The Ghost of Christmas Present touched Blitzen's leg and turned to smile at Francis. "Believing in what the world should be like is more difficult and more wonderful than most can fathom. Don't give up on us Christmas spirits so easily."

The big man guffawed loudly and disappeared. Blitzen lifted his head to see where the big man had gone. Even more amazing, he stood up and paced around where Present had just stood, sniffing the ground.

Francis laughed with a contagious mirth, jumping up and down. Soon Crosby was laughing as well, grabbing the boy for a hug. They both took turns patting Blitzen and allowing him to nuzzle their faces. The celebration was soon over, though, as they began getting ready for their flight to the North Pole. They climbed onto Blitzen's back, and once again they soared up into the sky.

12

The Glistening Gates
of A Make Believe Place

Flying this time felt like an entirely new experience. Francis' first flight had been at night. He had also spent much of the time worried about things chasing him. This flight was during daylight. The snow covered hills sparkled in the sunlight. It was beautiful.

Shortly after noon, Francis spotted what could only be a vast walled city. As they neared, he saw that the wall was ice, nearly twenty feet tall. There were pine trees and polar bears carved into the side of the wall. The gates were made from massive oak planks, painted red.

Blitzen landed a few yards in front of the gates and Crosby began to dismount. "Why didn't we just fly into the city?" Francis asked as he followed suit.

"There be magic that keeps things from flying in whenever they want to. Ya got to come through one of the gates if ya want to come in," Crosby answered as they approached the gate.

A hairy head poked out from atop the wall: "Who goes there?"

"Ya know darn well know who goes here. Open the gates!" Crosby called back.

"Croz, is that you?" The guard replied. He pulled his head back and they heard him shouting for other guards to open the gate. A great groaning noise came from the doors as they began to move. They slowly swung open, revealing the most beautiful city Francis had ever seen. The buildings were built from timber with green slate roofs. Intricately carved designs were on all the doors and window frames. Stunning shades of red, green, and gold were used to paint the homes and other buildings, and some of the buildings seemed to be built around enormously tall conifer trees.

The town was also filled with what Francis assumed were other elves. Surprisingly, Crosby seemed to be quite tall for an elf. They all seemed to be dressed in fur like Crosby. The elf women were generally more plump than human women, but they were all pretty. Most of the elf men wore beards as Crosby had said, but you could see that not all were warriors like Crosby. There were carpenters and stable hands, bakers and clerks. Many smiled at Crosby or shouted greetings to him.

Francis wasn't sure, but it seemed like all of the elves looked suspiciously at him. It was quite unsettling, but as Crosby didn't seem to notice, Francis continued to follow him. They meandered through streets and between buildings for some time, and Francis was continually amazed at everything he was seeing.

"Where are we going, Crosby? To your house?"

Crosby turned to look at Francis. A small smile crossed his face and he said, "We be going to see Santa, boy."

With that, they entered into a huge square. There was an enormous castle across from them. Thousands of elves were milling through the square, speaking with each other as they went about their business When they finally made it through the crowds to the entrance of the castle, carved reindeer encircled the door and several elf guards stood at attention. Crimson flags waved from the parapet. A bunch of holly leaves was the sigil on the field of the flag. As they approached the entrance, one of the guards nodded at Crosby, but other than that, none of them moved.

Francis followed Crosby into Santa's magic castle.

The Figment of Children's Imaginations

13

The front doors opened into a huge foyer. There were twin staircases, one on each side of the room. They walked straight through the foyer to a door in the center of the far wall. Crosby opened a door which lead them to a corridor that seemed to go on forever, their steps echoing around them. Dark-stained wood pillars and beams were spaced maybe eight feet apart, which made Francis feel as if he were walking through giant crochet wickets. The walls between the beams were decorated with elaborate tapestries depicting many different festive scenes: children opening gifts, a choir singing, snow falling on a tiny chapel in the woods. They were all expertly embroidered. As Francis glanced at each, he felt as if he were a part of the scene depicted.

As they neared the door at the end of the hallway, there were four large, framed paintings. At first glance, they each seemed to be of the same man. However, as Francis got closer, he saw that it was merely that the men all had similar features: large white beards, round cheeks, eyes that seemed to squint when they smiled. They were all decked in red cloth trimmed with white fur. Under each painting was a plaque that had each man's name and title. They read as follows:

Nicholas, the first Claus. The first follower of the One who brought joy to the world.

Tomte, the second Claus. The follower who tamed the wild reindeer to spread cheer.

Kris, the third Claus. The follower who brought the joy outside of Europe.

Ebenezer, the fourth Claus...

The final plaque did not have a description of the man's deeds. Since it was the last portrait, Francis assumed that this man was still serving his term. As he was studying the paintings, he heard a creak of hinges and turned to see the real life face of the man in the final painting. He was old but had an air of strength about him. He smiled at Francis and beckoned him and Crosby into the room.

The room was a cozy den with a fireplace; a roaring fire was engulfing a huge log. There was a workbench with a few different toys and parts haphazardly laying atop it. One wall was covered entirely with bookshelves full of various colored books. A warm scent of cinnamon and cranberries wafted through the air from a pot hanging over the fire. Santa grabbed a few mugs from a cart near the hearth and began ladling a deep golden liquid into each.

"Crosby, it seems it took you longer than we initially thought to bring this young man back," Santa said as he handed Francis a mug of mulled cider.

Crosby snorted, accepted his own mug, and said, "Aye, it did, Ebenezer, it did. We ran into a bit of trouble, but the boy is capable."

Santa turned to face Francis, who fidgeted under his gaze.

"The boy has the Gift," Crosby told Santa.

Santa did not turn his gaze from Francis, but his eyebrows rose in surprise. "So my supposition was correct it seems." Crosby nodded his head in agreement as Francis shrugged his shoulders, at a loss for what to say. "I trust you did not tell anyone else of this," Santa said to Crosby, raising his eyebrows to make the statement a question. Crosby nodded in agreement and took a deep draught from his mug.

"As meaningful as the arrival of the Gift is," Ebenezer said, "we must talk of that later. For now, there are some things you must know. I told you several days ago that I have been trying to find you, but I did not tell you why. It is because I believe, even more so now that I know you have the Gift, that you are meant to be the fifth Claus. Since the beginning of Christmas, there have only been - "

Francis spat out the mouth-full of cider he had just took in and gasped, "You think I'm going to be Santa Claus?!"

14

The Darkness and The Light

"I believe that is what is meant to be," Santa replied. "I am not privy to all the magics involved with the season of Yule, but I believe you were specially prepared for this task."

"But I'm just a kid," Francis complained.

"Ho ho ho!" Santa laughed. "I don't expect you to become the fifth Claus immediately, my boy. There will be years of training. I myself trained under the third Claus for nearly four decades. I was older than you when the mantel passed to me. They say old dogs can't learn new tricks, but I showed them... it just took me a long time! Ho ho ho!"

Francis became lost in thought about what this might mean for him. No more television, no more trampolines, no more soda. But there were good things about it too: he thought about having a stable home. He thought about always being near his friend Crosby. All sorts of scenarios were passing through Francis' mind when one very shocking realization occurred to him. "But I can't be the next Santa; I don't have a beard."

Crosby and Santa looked at each other and burst into laughter. "My boy, these things come in time. You are still shy of your thirteenth birthday. What's more important is that you understand the purpose of the advent season and why we bring joy to children."

"But you didn't bring me any joy last year," Francis muttered.

A somber look crossed Santa's face. "I know." He went over and laid a hand on Francis' shoulder. "Rauhen's power grows and he interferes with our work. I am sorry that you felt forgotten last year. It was not my intention. I am glad that you saw firsthand why we must continue our cause of spreading joy to children. No child should have to feel as you did last year. I pray you focus on that as we begin your training."

Francis looked Santa in the eye for a long moment, then nodded.

"Are you aware of the Humbugs?" Santa asked the boy. When Francis nodded, Santa continued. "Many years ago the first Humbug manifested itself. It made its way here and caused great harm." Santa paused to look at Crosby who was staring at the fire, avoiding Santa's eyes. He turned back to Francis and continued, "It took us some time to learn how to deal with them. Unfortunately, by the time we had figured out how to destroy them, there were too many for us to deal with quickly.

"Even more disturbing, the Humbugs began congregating several miles away from our city. Though the Humbugs themselves are mindless destroyers of joy, something strange happened when they gathered: some sort of sentient life form was created, one whom we now call Rauhen. He seems to have limited control over the Humbugs in that he can direct them where to go. Though he can't give them specific orders, just getting them near us is enough to cause great damage to our people and plans."

"What about the abominable snowmen? They seem like they can do exactly what he says," Francis asked.

Santa sighed. "One of my great failures as the Claus. The snowmen were a peaceful race that lived near the North Pole. They were very interested in our work but were not well suited for making toys or dealing with reindeer. In my thoughtlessness, I told them their services were not needed. This is not true: everyone should be - must be - involved with spreading Christmas cheer.

"They took my slight to heart and began stewing in anger. When Rauhen came into being, they were easily enticed to his side. They have been a thorn in our side ever since. They are dangerous foes, made even more so by the hatred in their hearts for us."

Francis thought about all that Santa had told him, then asked, "Can you defeat Rauhen?" Santa shook his head and Francis lowered his head in despair.

There was a long stretch of silence, then Santa spoke, "I believe that's why you are here, though. I think you can.

"I don't know much about Rauhen, but I know he does not want Christmas and the joy it brings to continue. If someone does not stand against him, this may very well be the last time I will be able to complete my task. And if I fail, I believe the line of Clauses will be finished."

Francis looked up to Santa and said, "How can I get ready?"

After their initial conversation, Francis was shown to a room all his own. An elf he had not yet met brought him a tray full of warm breads and spicy sausages with cranberries in them. He ate his fill and climbed into the large bed and pulled on the voluminous covers. He was asleep in moments.

Francis spent a few weeks working with Santa, learning how things were done in the North Pole. Santa was also preparing him for the Christmas Eve delivery. Santa seemed to think that Francis' understanding of how the lightbulbs worked was very important to the Christmas delivery, so Francis spent lots of time skating about and learning the inner-workings of trees.

He awoke late one morning to a knock on his door. Crosby was there with a smirk on his face: "Lazy day, is it?"

Francis let him in and said, "Usually someone wakes me, but I guess Santa decided I could have a day off. It does feel good to have slept in some." Francis began getting ready for the day. "What are we doing today?"

"Well, lad, I got plenty of things to do today. I thought ya might benefit from a bit of time with Blitzen."

"Yeah!" Francis exclaimed and raced out of the room. Crosby smiled to himself and followed after the boy. Francis was so excited that he got lost before realizing he had no idea how to get to the stable. After trying several different routes, Francis finally decided to ask someone for directions.

By the time he arrived, Crosby was waiting for him. "I could of tried to find ya, but I thought it might be more fun to see if'n ya could find your own way."

Francis gave the elf a light shove then asked, "Where's Blitzen?" With that, the huge reindeer walked out of the barn doors and gave Francis a nuzzle. Francis gripped Blitzen's snout and laughed.

"Well, boy, I'll be leaving ya two to yer own designs – don't break nothing." And with that, Crosby walked away whistling a jaunty tune.

Blitzen was already saddled, so Francis climbed up and gave the animal a light kick. Blitzen took off running. It was definitely exciting to fly on the animal, but it was equally amazing riding atop him as he ran on the ground. He was just so fast.

They ran around the stable yard for a while, and then Blitzen took off into the sky. They flew over the buildings and soon they were over the wall. There appeared to be no magic that kept things from flying out of the city wall, only in. They flew over thick forests and a frozen lake. There were hills and valleys. Finally, Blitzen took them down to an empty clearing in the middle of a dense forest.

Upon landing, Blitzen took a few steps, then laid down on the ground. He turned his head to the side so he could see Francis, and waited. Francis stared back for a moment, then dismounted. "Why are we here, Blitzen?"

Blitzen got up and walked over to a tuft of grass and began munching. After he had a bite, he looked at Francis and nodded to something behind him, a bit to the right. Francis turned to look and was startled to see a figure standing behind him. She was shorter than he was, dressed in a Victorian era child's nightgown. More shocking than her appearance was the fact that she was translucent, much like the Humbugs. When he noticed this, Francis jumped back in fright and called for Blitzen to make his escape.

But Blitzen just looked up at him, chewing his grass. He blinked lazily, then leaned back down for another bite. Francis began to run towards the reindeer but stopped when he heard a voice in his head: "Stop this nonsense! I will not hurt you. Turn to me and listen."

Francis slowly turned. She was not glowing purple at least. In fact, she had a pleasant golden glow to her. Francis took several cautious steps towards her and said, "Who are you?"

"Many refer to me as the Ghost of Christmas Past. I am the keeper of the knowledge of past Christmases." Her mouth never moved. She never blinked. She just stared at him. He did not hear the words so much as he felt them in his mind. "I am here to inform you of the purpose of the foci you have discovered."

"Foci? You mean the box with the lightbulbs? You know how they work?!"

"Of course. I know all things that are related to past Christmases."

"Cool! But I think I figured it out."

"You have figured out very little of the foci. I have seen you fumbling with them like a child with a puzzle. The foci are not toys to taunt that unshaven oaf with, they are to help you harness the magics of Christmas."

"Magics of Christmas? You mean flying around and delivering presents?"

Her face darkened in annoyance, though her mouth still never moved: "Winter, Warmth, Life, and Right."

"That's four... but I've only had three different light bulbs." Francis mused aloud.

"The fourth focus is golden hued. This is the only magic you seem to have any natural aptitude in. When you called my associate Present, you did so without the aid of the focus of Right. Impressive in spite of your bumbling attempts at learning the others. Now open the receptacle and we shall work on learning the other foci as well."

"But I didn't bring it with me; it's back on the desk in my room." Francis complained.

"It is behind you."

Francis turned to look, but saw nothing. He looked back at Past inquisitively. She nodded at him to go get the box. Confused he turned and took a few steps scanning the clearing for the Gift. On his third step he tripped on something under the snow and hit the ground face first. He got himself up on his knees and wiped the snow from his face. When he dug in the snow to see what he had tripped over, he was shocked to see his carved box. He looked up at Past with an incredulous look.

She stared back at him with a hint of a smile at the corner of her mouth.

16. The Lessons of The Past

Past was an effective teacher, but she did not tolerate silliness. When Francis pulled the blue bulb from his box and began skating around, she somehow stopped the effect of the bulb and Francis went tumbling across the ground. "There will be time for recreation at another time," she informed Francis. "Magic is meant to aid you in controlling your environment for the benefit of others, not your amusement. The magic of Winter is not only a boon to the Claus' spreading of merriment; it can also be an effective tool in the struggle with Rauhen."

"You mean because I can throw snowballs at him?"

"Yes..." He heard in his mind. Her face had that annoyed look again. "Though that does not seem to be an effective weapon against an immaterial being.

"One could hide oneself from sight within a heavy snowfall. The snow on the ground could be used to propel the feet of your mount forward while slowing your pursuer. You must use your mind to figure out the best use of magic for your situation. It is not always the most obvious."

Francis listened intently to Past for several hours, learning as much as he could of the magics of Winter, Warmth, and Life. When she seemed pleased with his understanding of those, she spoke: "You finally have a good understanding of the basic uses of the foci. As you progress further in your knowledge, you will no longer need the foci to aid you; the magics will become a part of you.

"However, know this: the more your powers grow, the more your predecessor's fade. Learn from him, as he is wiser than you. Do as he says, but aid him, for his work will not yet be finished though you gain his power.

"We have completed what lessons need to be learned. Though the future of Christmas does not rest solely on your shoulders alone, you are vital to its continued existence. Be valiant and steadfast. Farewell."

With that she disappeared. Francis stood there for a moment, waiting for some other information. He looked around, not believing she had truly left so abruptly. Finally, he shouted, "But what about the magic of Right?"

He did not see her again, but he heard her words in his head: "You need no further instruction in knowing how to believe in what should be. Believe more strongly if you wish to excel in the magic of Right." She spoke no more, even though he called out other questions. Receiving no more answers, he walked over to Blitzen and patted the beast, who had laid down for a nap some time ago. "I suppose you were in on this the whole time." Blitzen stared at him for a moment, then nodded. Francis shook his head in surprise.

"Can you talk, too?" Blitzen gave him what could only be described as a disparaging look. "It wouldn't surprise me, especially with all the other weird stuff I've seen these past few weeks," Francis said and climbed up onto the saddle. Blitzen stood up and stretched his legs. He walked in a slow circle a few times then took off running across the clearing. He jumped in the air and just barely cleared the tops of the trees as they rose into the sky. "Cutting it a little close to those trees, weren't you?" Francis teased the reindeer. Blitzen just bleated in annoyance and flew on.

Francis did his best to create a winter wind to help carry them back to the city more quickly. Without the use of the bulb, Francis was not sure if he created a wind or not. However, he was not comfortable enough flying to take his hands off the reigns to try and get the blue bulb out of the box. Still, it did seem as if their return trip was shorter than their trip out.

When they returned to the stable, one of the guards told Francis that Crosby wanted to see him and that he was probably in the kitchens. Francis got directions and thanked him.

Crosby was enjoying a large slice of ham and mashed potatoes when Francis found him. "Have an eventful day, did ya? You and Blitzen was gone for some time."

Francis told him all about his lessons with Past.

"I can't imagine ya had a lick of fun; Past don't waste time," Crosby responded when Francis was done with his recounting. "It sounds like ya had a day full of thinking, what say ya that we go out tomorrow and find some more timber for the workshop? They be nearly done with their toy making, but could use a bit more wood."

"That sounds great, Crosby." Not only did Francis want to spend some time with Crosby, but he thought some time out in the open would give him an opportunity to work on his control of the magics.

Francis ate dinner with Crosby and they shared stories about their lives. By the time Francis got back to his room, he was exhausted and ready for sleep.

The Timber That Led Them Away

The next morning Francis was ready to go when Crosby knocked on his door. He had decided against bringing his wooden box as it would mean that he would have to work the magics without the foci. He still dressed warmly, just in case he wasn't able to keep himself as toasty as he would like with the magic of Warmth.

"I think me and you'll scout out the best trees, leave a trail back to the main gate for the loggers to find them," Crosby told Francis. "We'll needs to walk a ways, as they're always cutting down trees for wood." Francis liked the sound of that. The longer he was out in the open, the more time he would have to practice his magic.

They left through the main gate after a large breakfast of eggs and bacon. The bacon had a crust of nutmeg cooked around the edges, which was much better than Francis had expected. He also drank four glasses of egg nog. The chaperones at the boys home never allowed them to have more than one glass of egg nog, and that only on Christmas morning. Francis was also able to filch a couple of gingerbread cookies fresh from the oven from one of the bakers. It was a wonderful meal, and Francis felt more than ready to hike for the day. Crosby acquired some dried sausages and biscuits for their midday meal.

They left through the main gate that Francis had first entered the city through three days ago. Though it was below freezing outside, the sky was bright and clear. "Which direction are we going, Crosby?" Francis asked.

"Which direction? We be at the north pole, lad. Every direction we could go be south. The best way to tell ya which direction we be going is to say 'this way'." Crosby pointed in front of them and laughed. Francis smiled too. This was going to be a fun day.

As they walked, Francis tried to fling a snowball from his empty hand. Nothing happened. After an hour or so of intermittently tossing nothing, he thought back to what it felt like to use the blue lightbulb to fling the snowball. He focused on that feeling and was surprised when instead of nothing coming from his hand, a spray of flurry-like snow flew out. It wasn't controlling the mighty winds of Winter, but it was a start. Crosby had been watching the whole time, keeping his mouth shut. When Francis produced the flurry, he gave a round of applause, muffled by his fur gloves.

The flurry was fun, but his arm was getting a bit tired. He thought next he might try making his toes feel warm. He thought that would be simpler than trying to create something from nothing, and he was right. He imagined his toes warm and almost instantaneously they were. Francis smiled to himself. This magic thing was turning out to be pretty useful.

"How far do you think we'll have to go until we get to some good trees?" Francis asked.

"Might be another four hours," Crosby responded.

That seemed like a long time to Francis. He began thinking about how his magic might help them travel faster. He thought he might be able to make the bottom of his feet icy again, so that he might skate. But that would leave Crosby far behind him.

Suddenly Francis stopped in his tracks. Crosby turned: "Problem, boy?" Francis smiled, but shook his head. Crosby shrugged, turned, took a step, and promptly slipped and fell.

Francis laughed as he began skating around the confused elf. "I thought maybe we could travel faster if we skated. Instead of making just my feet icy, I made an icy path in front of us so both of us could skate. Pretty neat, huh?"

Crosby smirked, "Aye, lad, it be neat. Next time, warn me. You might accidentally get snow on ya." Crosby reached up for a hand to get up. As soon as he was upright, he pulled Francis close and slid a large chunk of icy snow down the back of his shirt. Crosby then began gracefully - surprisingly - skating down the path Francis had made, chuckling to himself.

Francis shook the snow out of his shirt and caught up to Crosby. It was not hard to make an icy path, but he did need to constantly turn another 50 feet in front of them to ice. He only forgot once. Hitting the regular snow sent them sprawling, and Francis thought that he had enough snow down his shirt. Also, Crosby whacked him on the arm every once in awhile to remind him.

They traveled for a few more hours until they came to a massive cliff face. It was so tall, it was hard to see the top of the cliff. Crosby noticed that to one side of the cliff face was a cluster of tall and wide trees, perfect for cutting lumber from. They decided this was a perfect place to mark for the loggers to come back to. They put their packs down and busied themselves getting their meal ready. "How do they get the trees back to the city from this far away?" Francis asked.

"Them reindeer are strong. Ya get four of them together and they can pull a tree back to the gates from here in less time then it took us to get here." Crosby began picking up some kindling as he talked. "I know our food don't need no cooking, but I thought you might like to try starting a fire with yer hocus pocus." Crosby gave the boy a wink and started stacking the kindling.

They sat around the pile of wood and began opening their food. After a few bites, Francis began trying to set the stack on fire with his magic. He tried to transfer the warm feeling he could make in his feet to the pile of wood. After several minutes, a small wisp of smoke rose from the wood. Francis let out a "Whoop!" and jumped up in triumph. He turned to share his joy with Crosby, only to see the elf standing and looking behind them.

Maybe 30 yards away from them was a large group of snowmen, walking steadily towards them.

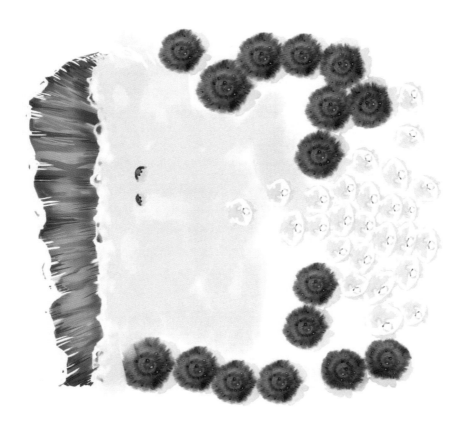

The Unknowable Future

The color drained from Francis's face as he saw the horde of abominable snowmen. Crosby pulled out Ol' Ironhead, but Francis had no weapon to protect himself. "What are we going to do?" He frantically asked Crosby.

"Don't know, lad, but now would be a good time to master some of that magic you been working on," Crosby replied.

As they neared, Francis began to fling his arm at the mob. A few tufts of flurry flew out, finally followed by a few well-formed snowballs. The last one sailed in a long slow arc and actually struck one of the far-off snowmen in the chest. However, with his thick fur, he did not seem to notice. "Boy, they're called 'snowmen'. Yer not going to frighten them off with some snowballs. Try fire."

Francis and Crosby began backing up, their backs to the cliff face. They were completely surrounded now with no possible route of escape. The snowmen slowed as they neared. Francis wanted to panic but remembered the last time he and Crosby had been in trouble. He did not want to get slapped before dying at the hands of a mob of vicious snowmen so he calmed himself and thought.

Francis held his hand out and focused on the magic of Warmth. With the snowmen approaching, he had quite the incentive to focus. He stared at the palm of his hand, a line of sweat trickled down his brow. Suddenly, a tiny tongue of flame sprouted from his hand, the size of a candle flame. Francis believed in the fire until it was the size of an apple. He looked up at the approaching mob and hurled it at the nearest snowman. It struck the creature on its upper thigh and began burning its thick, white fur.

The beast let out a horrid, gravelly screech and began beating the flames out with his massive hands. Other snowmen walked around the burning one and closed the gap.

Francis lost the will to fight at that moment. There were so many snowmen approaching, he would not be able to burn them all. Not before some of them got to him and Crosby. Francis backed up until his back hit the cliff face. Crosby was swinging his hammer at any of the snowmen that came too near, but it was hopeless – there were too many of the creatures.

Francis began to cry. He did not want to die. He did not want to let Santa down. Most importantly, he did not want to let the other children of the world down. He feared that if he died, Christmas may end as well. Francis was trying to wipe his eyes so he could see, when a large shrouded figure walked out of the cliff face to his right.

It was taller than Present had been, but nowhere near as brightly dressed. It wore a hooded robe of some sort, dark gray. The robe seemed to be covered in black smears of soot. The being raised its hand and gestured across the border of snowmen.

They all froze in place.

He pointed a finger towards the crowd of snowmen; the hand was gnarled and twisted at one moment, then smooth and straight the next. It never seemed to stay one way, always changing appearance. Where it pointed, a path was cleared through the crowd of snowmen; any portion of a snowman that was in the path melted away. A few were totally gone, while others were missing limbs or half of their bodies. It was a grisly sight.

Francis looked into the shadowy hood in shock. He could not see a face in the darkness, but he distinctly heard a wispy voice whisper, "Go."

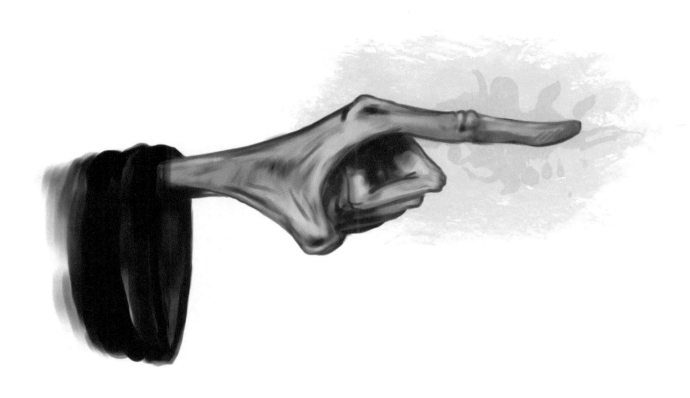

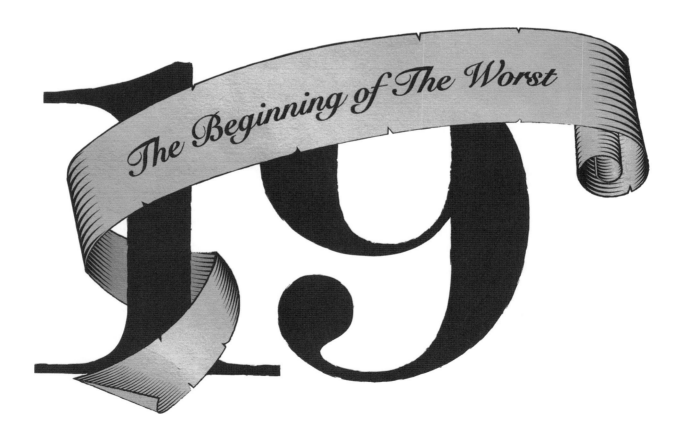

The Beginning of The Worst

Francis took off immediately. He was not sure who was more frightening: the horde of snowmen, or the thing that apparently had just saved them. At first, as he ran through the midst of the snowmen, he noticed that though they were not moving, their eyes were following him. As he neared the end, some were able to turn their heads as well.

After they made it through unharmed, Crosby said, "Lad, I don't think they're gonna stay frozen for much longer. Ya up to making one of them ice paths again?"

Francis looked and saw that several were turning their whole torsos towards them. He turned back and focused. After a few seconds he nodded and took a tentative sliding step. The path was ready. They took off down the path, skating as fast as they could. Shortly after the horde was out of sight, they began to hear guttural howls coming from behind them.

They traveled for hours, due north. Though the howls became more distant and eventually trailed off, they knew they were being followed. When they finally saw the walls of the city, Francis felt a great sense of relief wash over him. They would be safe behind those thick walls.

When they reached the gates Crosby shouted up: "Open the gates! We got snowmen hunting us!"

"Snowmen? Where!?" a young guard called down.

"Open the gates or I'll give ya a thrashing you'll never forget!"

"Yes sir! Right away! Let me go get some help." With that, the young watch elf ran off. Crosby grumbled to himself in frustration at having to wait. Then he turned to look at Francis. "Boy, this ain't normal, all these snowmen congregating like that. I think something bad be about to happen. When we get in, go and find Ebenezer and tell him what happened. With it being Christmas Eve tomorrow, I think we can be certain those snowmen will be coming here. I need to inform the head guard."

Howls began to slowly reach their ears as Crosby spoke. An older grizzled guard came to the wall then. His face looked distraught as he stared into the distance towards the sound. "The lad's getting some help to open the gate, Croz. Should be up in a moment," the older guard called down to them. With that the gate began opening and they walked through and separated, each to complete their own task.

It took looking in several places, but Francis finally found Santa in the main kitchen. He told the bearded man all that had happened when he and Crosby were out that they. Santa's face grew more and more concerned. When Francis got to the part of the tale when the shrouded figure showed up, Santa's eyebrows raised in surprise. "Future saved you?" Santa asked, more to himself than to Francis.

"Future? That was the Ghost of Christmas Future? That guy was really scary." Francis said.

Santa smiled at Francis. "There is always something unsettling about the unknown. However, the fact that he stepped in to save you means that you or Crosby are important to the future of Christmas. It is his job to save future Christmases. Though he does not intervene often, it is always telling when he does."

"What does it tell us?" Francis asked.

"I believe it confirms just how important you are, though it could be Crosby to be sure. I can truthfully say, though, I need you if I have any hope of delivering the toys this year. I think it's wonderful that you are growing in your understanding of the Christmas magics, but as your power grows, my own control of the magics is diminished. We must work as a team now to complete the Christmas delivery. You must become my apprentice. Are you ready for this responsibility?" Santa looked kindly at Francis, but Francis could see that he, and the whole world, were counting on Francis to help.

"I am, sir." Francis said. "Is there anything I can do right now to help?"

"Tomorrow will be a big day, why don't you get something to eat and then call it a night?" Santa suggested.

That sounded like a good idea to Francis. Santa's sense of calm helped Francis feel relieved. He ate a big dinner and went to his room. He undressed and fell fast asleep, forgetting about the snowmen that were outside of the city.

Francis was startled awake by a banging on his door. "Get up, lad! Get up!" Bleary-eyed, Francis stumbled to the door and lifted the latch. Crosby was there, hammer in one hand, the other raised to knock again.

"What? It's still dark out, it can't be time to get up." Francis sleepily complained.

"It's near to noon, boy. They've blotted out the sun. Santa's at the sleigh. His guard wouldn't let him come get you; it be too dangerous. He needs you on the sleigh."

"Noon? On the sleigh soon? Crosby, what's going on?"

"No time, boy! Get dressed and bring the Gift!" Crosby hurried Francis into his room and starting pulling his sleep shirt off of him.

"Stop, Crosby! I can do it myself. There can't possibly be this big of a rush if it's not even noon." Crosby harumphed, but kept his mouth shut otherwise. Francis was soon dressed, with the box in hand. "I'm ready."

Crosby let out a big sigh and then stepped into the hall. Francis had to nearly run to keep up with the elf, who was clearly agitated. When they reached the door to the outside, Crosby stopped Francis with a hand on his chest. "Don't ya worry about them Humbugs, they can't get passed the walls into the city; there's barrier spells woven into the walls. Stay close to me, but keep an eye out for snowmen. We need to get ya to Ebenezer at the stable, else he won't be able to deliver the gifts." Crosby eyed Francis.

"Are you ready, lad?" he asked.

Crosby's frantic nature had finally registered in Francis' mind. He felt frantic himself, but not knowing what the situation truly was like, he took a deep breath and nodded at Crosby. With that, Crosby adjusted his grip on his hammer and kicked open the door.

It was not the same place Francis had seen before. The sky was dark as Crosby had said. Several buildings were on fire and small packs of snowmen were fighting bands of elves. Many of the elves were armed with axes or cudgels. A few even had swords that appeared to be crafted from narwal tusks. They were skilled warriors, but the snowmen were generally twice the size of the elves, if not more, and they seemed to be just as used to battle.

Crosby locked eyes with Francis and then nodded. They took off running, heading towards a small alley between the kitchens and another residential building. One snowman happened to notice them and broke away from his current battle to meet them. He roared when he met them, but Crosby smashed his knee with his hammer; the large beast fell to the ground howling in pain, unable to give chase.

They reached the alley and stopped in the darkest part to hide for a moment. As they had been running, Francis had noticed that Humbugs were indeed circling the entire wall of the city. They were not coming in, but they were also not letting anyone out.

"What happened?" Francis whispered.

"That group of snowmen we met up with earlier must of found some friends. They showed up round sunrise. Shortly after, this oily cloud appeared up in the sky. When it got therk enough, them Humbugs started flying up. While we was focused on the Humbugs, the snowmen started bashing down the gate. If ya ask me, I don't think it was no coincidence that we ran into that gang of them out there. I think this was planned."

Changing the subject, Crosby said, "See them tall trees over there? Those are the trees that circle the stable. Ebenezer's in there with the sleigh. Fortunately, we got the darn thing all loaded last night, so it's ready to go. We just got to get ya in somehow."

Crosby led the way through the alley. The street that it opened up onto was pretty quiet. A few elves were hurriedly trying to get off the street, but there were no snowmen. Crosby led them quickly down the street. They did their best to stay in the shadows, slipping from doorways to alleyways. After several tense moments, they reached the square that the stable was in. It was surrounded by armed elves doing their best to fight off the snowmen that were surrounding them.

The stable door was open and the most heavily guarded. If they could slip past the snowmen, they should have no problem getting into the stable.

"We got a chance here, boy. Those snowmen ain't paying no attention to us, so we'll try and slip by them. If there's an opening, you go, even if I can't follow ya right then, you understand?"

Francis nodded, more intent on the swarming mass in front of them.

"Look at me, boy! Do ya understand?!"

Francis stared at him: "I understand."

"Let's go." Crosby said, and took off towards the open stable door. Francis hesitated at first, then ran after him. When they got to the rear of the snowmen, Crosby hit one of them in the back so hard, he flew into another five feet in front of him and they both collapsed to the ground.

Crosby began shouting and swinging wildly at snowmen. They soon took notice of the elf and many turned to face him. He batted several away with his hammer while others skipped back from his swings. More and more snowmen were turning to Crosby, opening up a path to the stable.

Crosby began shouting challenges at the snowmen, laughing triumphantly every time his hammer met one of them. When the path was totally open, Crosby stopped laughing, and shouted to Francis: "Go, lad, you can make it!"

Francis took off towards the door, hearing the clash of battle all around him. When he passed through the guards and into the stable, he looked back to watch for Crosby.

Crosby was nowhere to be seen. There was only a big pile of snowmen thrashing wildly.

The Air Beneath The Hoofs

21

"Where's Crosby?" Francis asked no one, even though he knew. "Crosby? Crosby?! CROSBY!" Francis ran back towards the open door, but was restrained by some of the other elves there.

A warm hand rested on his shoulder. Francis looked up through tears to see Santa standing by his side. Santa squeezed his shoulder reassuringly and smiled sadly. "Don't ever forget the gift your friend gave you, Francis. Not everyone receives such a special gift given freely.

"I don't mean to rush your mourning, but we must attempt to leave if we are to have any hope of spreading joy this year." Santa patted Francis on the back and walked towards his sleigh. The reindeer were already hitched to the sleigh. Several elves in full armor were astride other of the massive reindeer. Their weapons were in hand.

Santa began checking the harness on each reindeer. As he did so, he gave each reindeer something to eat from his pocket. He spoke quietly to each, patted their flanks or scratched behind their ears. When he was done, he put a hand on his sleigh and turned to Francis. "It is cruel that what you had just gained was taken away so swiftly, but we are not capable of changing what has been done..."

"Past could change this, couldn't she?!" Francis interrupted.

"Truthfully, I do not know. And if she could, I do not know that she would. The Ghosts do as they will, and their will is to protect Christmas. What we desire is not always what is best for Christmas. I believe the best we can do is hope for the return of the child whose arrival started this season of giving. When that happens, all things will be right again. Until then, we are tasked with making the world as right as possible."

Francis listened to Santa's words. He thought of his life. He thought of his loneliness growing up without friends. Without love. Without joy. If there were another boy or girl living like that, he would feel sad for them. Now that he had magic powers, he would help them.

Francis looked up at Santa's face. "I don't want any more kids to have to live like I did. I want to start by giving them a great Christmas morning. Can we give every kid a great Christmas morning?"

Santa looked Francis in the eye: "...I don't know. If there's a chance, I need your help."

Francis nodded and climbed into the sleigh. He set the Gift down on the center of the bench and opened it. Inside was the golden bulb. He picked it up and it glowed brightly. Santa climbed into the sleigh and grabbed the reigns. "Are you ready?" He asked the reindeer and elves. They all nodded.

"On Dasher! On Dancer! On Prancer and Vixen! On Comet! On Cupid! On Donder and Blitzen!" The mounted elves took off, unencumbered by a sleigh. Those pulling the sleigh began picking up speed as they approached the door. The elves on foot parted for the mounted ones and the sleigh, showing a huge group of snowmen waiting for them. When the mounted elves left the stable, they began swinging their axes and cudgels, clearing the way for Santa's sleigh. When the sleigh reached the door, Francis saw that the massive pines that circled the stable were slapping snowmen with their branches.

Santa held the reigns with one hand and directed heavy gusts of Winter wind, blowing even more snowmen out of the way than he had already done with the trees. "To the top of the wall!" Santa bellowed and the reindeer leapt into the air, pulling the sleigh up with them.

Francis clutched the golden lightbulb and watched as the sleigh neared the wall of Humbugs waiting for them.

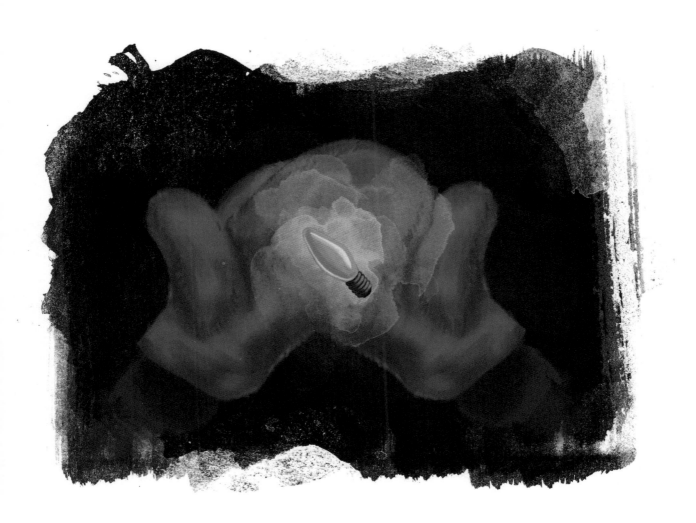

22.

The Golden Light of Right

As they hurtled towards the Humbugs, Santa lifted his free hand towards them. "The Humbugs are cold, empty creatures. You can't stop them with Winter or anything physical that Life can create. But Warmth, that's a different story." When they were nearly upon the Humbugs, Santa unleashed a lance of fire from his outstretched hand. Shrill shrieks erupted from the Humbugs then went silent as the flame disintegrated the ghouls. The magnitude of Santa's control over the magics of Christmas was staggering. Moving all those tree limbs at once, forcing winter gales, flaming streams of fire; Francis was lucky if he could throw out a single fireball. He had much to learn.

The sleigh flew through the opening in the line of Humbugs and Francis let out a whoop of victory. The sleigh was flying, faster and faster, leaving the chaos of the city behind them. Francis looked behind them to see if they were being followed.

Some of the Humbugs had turned to give chase, but many were being pulled into a dark purple mass that was growing with each humbug that was pulled into it, turning darker and darker until it was nearly black. The mass began flying towards them, pulling Humbugs into itself as it came, growing larger. Angry piercing yellow eyes opened on the mass and a toothy mouth appeared, unable to close because of all the teeth.

"Santa..." Francis said as he grabbed Santa's arm. The man looked down at Francis and then behind them. His face grew grave.

"Francis, Rauhen is coming for us. I don't believe I can stop him. Your control of Right has become so great, that I barely have any left. I need you to believe and make this Right."

They lurched as the huge face tried to bite the sleigh. The gaping maw bit down again, pulling a small piece of carved scrollwork off of the back of the sleigh. "Hurry, Francis!" Santa shouted.

Francis turned to face Rauhen. He grasped the golden bulb in both hands and began to believe as hard as he could that Christmas would be wonderful for every little boy and girl. The face let out a shriek and fell back twenty feet. Its eyes glowed brighter, angrier. It snarled and flew at them again. This time it took a massive bite out of the back of the sleigh, toys went spilling into the air behind them.

Santa put a warm hand on Francis' shoulder and smiled kindly. "You can do it, son."

The joy of being called 'son' filled Francis' heart and he believed that Rauhen should not exist. The face yowled and fell far behind them. Francis believed again, and the face split into hundreds of Humbugs for a moment, before Rauhen could pull itself back together.

Francis took all of his anger and discontent at being alone and mistreated and put it into his belief. The golden bulb glowed brighter than ever. It grew warm until it was nearly too hot to hold. Francis looked down at the bulb and smiled. He cocked his arm back and hurled the golden bulb at Rauhen. It sailed in a straight line, growing brighter and brighter until it struck the face where it's nose should have been.

Rauhen never made a noise. Humbugs began falling away from the mass, and then turning into purple clouds of mist that blew away. The face grew more and more misshapen as more of the ghouls fell off and blew away. Finally, there was one last Humbug. It looked Francis in the eye and pointed. Then a strong gust blew it away into dust.

Francis collapsed on the bench, next to Santa. He felt exhausted. He was glad to have defeated Rauhen, but saddened by the thought that they had lost most of the presents. He looked back at the damaged, nearly empty sleigh, and sighed.

"What's the matter, son?" Santa asked Francis.

"I wanted to get presents to all the kids, but he knocked most of them off the sleigh." Francis said.

Santa looked back at the wreckage. He smiled and looked down at Francis. "You might want to look again."

Francis was confused, but looked back anyway. The sleigh was as if nothing had ever happened to it. The gifts were once again stacked neatly in a huge pile. There was a slight rustle beneath the gifts, and Present lifted his face out of the pile. He gave Francis a wink, and then sunk back into the pile.

Francis and Santa flew off into the sky, heading for the Line Islands where the sun was already beginning to set on Christmas Eve.

The Delivery

23

It was hard to figure out how time worked for Santa that night as they delivered the toys. It would be safe to say that time froze as they delivered toys throughout each city. However, there was also an eerie lack of life. There were no humans out, no vehicles on the streets. There weren't even animals out. Every once in awhile, though, their would be a wind, but only a few leaves on trees would move, not all.

While they were traveling between houses, Santa asked Francis to fill the sack with the packages for the upcoming house. "I can't do that," Francis said, "I don't know which presents go to which house."

"Son, you might be surprised by what you know. Give it a try." Santa replied.

So Francis hopped in back of the sleigh and opened up the empty bag. He looked at the pile of presents and was drawn to a long, green gift. He picked it up and put it in the sack. That felt right. Then he saw a blue package with a white ribbon that seemed to match what he had already put in the bag. He filled the sack up with the packages that felt right to him. When they landed on the next house, Francis asked, "Is this right, Santa?"

Santa reached back and took the bag from Francis. He closed his eyes for moment, then said, "It feels perfect to me." Santa gave him a smile, then began walking towards the chimney. Santa did not climb down the chimney like Francis had always thought. Instead, as Santa neared the chimney he and the bag began to dematerialize until he was a sparkly mist of red, green, blue, and golden colors. That cloud swirled down the chimney. Several moments later, the cloud returned and formed back into Santa Claus.

"You're somehow using all four of the Christmas magics to travel into homes, is that right?" Francis inquired.

"Very observant of you, Francis. To be fair, I have been using all for the entire time, but it's a bit more apparent when I transport into homes. Would you like to come in with me at the next home?"

"Sure, I guess. I'll have to learn sometime, won't I?"

"That's true," Santa said as he climbed back into the sleigh. He snapped the reigns and the sleigh took off. When they landed on the next home, Francis handed Santa the newly filled sack and climbed out of the sleigh with the man. They walked to the chimney and Santa placed his hand on Francis' shoulder.

When he turned into the mist, Francis' sensory experience changed. He was no longer limited to only seeing where his eyes were looking or hearing only what sounds were most apparent. He saw every direction at once and comprehended it. Every noise was perceptible. Every scent, every taste, every physical feeling – they were all there in Francis' mind. He felt the gritty texture of the bricks as they flowed down the chimney. They smelled of oak and hickory smoke, pine and ash. They passed the glowing embers, still blazing hot, and materialized as themselves in a living room.

Francis was a little shocked to be only using his senses in a traditional way once again. As Santa went about placing the presents beneath the tree, Francis stood readjusting to his physical form.

When Santa was finished, they traveled back up to the sleigh. As they sat down, Francis finally spoke: "Is that how you know if they're naughty or nice?"

Santa nodded.

"I don't know if I like that," Francis said.

Santa nodded again, and seemed as if he was thinking of what to say. Several moments later he said, "I don't believe it's meant to be pleasant. But when children are aware that their actions are being watched and that they still receive gifts even when they are naughty, that is a wonderful thing. That is the essence of Christmas: a wonderful gift was given to people who do not deserve it. That is why I now give gifts to those who do not deserve them. It's a constant reminder of what we celebrate at Christmas time."

Francis thought on that the rest of the night.

The Life Francis Is Given

As Francis and Santa flew north, the sun began to rise. The light shimmered off the snow that covered the land surrounding the northernmost city in the world. Santa guided the sleigh towards the stable yard. Thousands of the inhabitants of the city had come out to see Santa's return. Many of them were dirty and had bandages on or wore slings.

A cry went up when they landed. Congratulatory handshakes were given, as well as a few kisses on their cheeks. Those made Francis blush. One particular elf maiden, Noel he thought her name was, did not seem to be much older than him. She was also very pretty. She smiled at him after she kissed his cheek. It made Francis feel funny. He would have to keep an eye on her.

There was a huge celebration with food and dancing and singing. It went on for several hours, well into the afternoon. When the party finally began to wind down, Francis found his way to his room. He took his clothes off and dressed for bed. He crawled in bed and quickly fell asleep. He had been awake all day and all night after all.

A bell tolled once, deep and resonant. It woke Francis up. He sat up in the dark, groggily rubbing his eyes.

"You did well," a familiar wispy whisper said.

Francis sat back hard against his headboard, startled by the voice.

As his eyes adjusted to the dark, Francis saw a tall, hooded figure standing in the corner. It did not move. "You will continue your education under Ebenezer. You will learn from him and you will eventually be given the title of Claus. You will suffer hardship and much pain. But you will persevere because I have chosen you to carry on the Claus through a very tumultuous time. I have been preparing you for this role your entire life. Every hardship you have suffered was meant to prepare you for what lies ahead. Remember your pain and desire to save others from that difficult life."

"You put me in that orphanage? Did you take my parents? Did you make the other boys be so mean to me?" Francis questioned the spirit.

"Persevere," it said and melted into the walls.

Francis sat in dark, thinking about what Future had said to him. He thought on it until his windows began to lighten with the rising sun. Francis got up and got dressed. He got a hardy breakfast, then found Santa in his den.

"What more can you teach me?" Francis asked.

"So much, son. So much." Santa said.

About

The Author

Joseph M. Bubenik has cultivated a love of Christmas since he was a boy. His insatiable hunger for anything having to do with the holiday season prompted him to create his own story. Though having desired to begin writing for some time, this is Joe's first book.

Joe is a lifelong resident of St. Louis, Missouri, where he lives with his wife Ali, and their three children, Evelynne, Remington, & Tiberius. He lives in a home that was built in the late 1800s.

Joe is a member of the St. Louis Beard & Mustache Club.

The Illustrator

Jeremy D. Plemon is an artist that enjoys working in many mediums. From oil paintings to digital designs, Jeremy creates pieces that range from humorous to emotionally impressive. Jeremy spends much of his time designing and creating hand-drawn signs for an organic grocery store.

Jeremy grew up in southern Illinois, but now resides with his wife Erin and their two children, Eliza and Reese, in St. Louis, Missouri. Their home is warm and inviting, especially during the holidays when he and his wife's knack for decorating really shines.

Made in the USA
San Bernardino, CA
25 November 2013